Produced by Kroha Associates, Inc.
Middletown, Connecticut.

Printed in the United States of America.

ISBN 1-56326-101-4

Disney Books By Mail offers a selection of entertaining
audio and video programs. For more information, write:
Disney Books By Mail, P.O. Box 11440, Des Moines, Iowa 50336

The Rainy-Day Picnic

By Ruth Lerner Perle

One April day, Daisy, Clarabelle, and Penny were at Minnie's house.

"What shall we play?" Daisy asked.

"I don't know," Clarabelle said. "There's nothing to do."

"Nothing at all!" Penny agreed.

Minnie looked out of the window. The cherry tree in front of her house was starting to blossom and the robins were busy building their nests.

"I know!" Minnie said. "It's spring! Time to have a picnic!"

"A picnic! A picnic!" everybody shouted. "Let's have a picnic!"

I'm so glad my friends like my idea. I hope we'll have a good time, don't you?

"Let's get our picnic lunch together," Minnie suggested.
"Good idea!" cried Daisy. "This is going to be so much fun!"

Everybody went to the kitchen to help. Daisy made peanut butter and jelly sandwiches. Clarabelle prepared fresh lemonade. Penny peeled carrots and made celery sticks. Minnie packed some cheese, cookies, and oranges.

The girls put the food in a big wicker basket together with paper plates, napkins, cups, and straws.

As they rolled up the picnic blanket, they listened to the weather report.

"It's going to be a lovely day today," the weather reporter said. "A good day to enjoy the warm spring sunshine."

"That's terrific!" Daisy said. "We've picked the perfect day for our picnic!"

Minnie took the picnic basket and Daisy grabbed her new camera. Penny took a ball to play with and Clarabelle brought her jump rope. "I think we have everything we need now," Minnie said.

"Yay! Let's go!" everybody shouted. They ran down the front steps and off to the picnic grounds.

When they arrived at the picnic grounds, the girls found a perfect spot right under a big birch tree.

Daisy spread out the blanket while Minnie unpacked the lunch basket.

"This was a good idea," Clarabelle said. "It feels great to be outdoors."

Penny threw the ball up in the air. "Come on, girls! Let's play ball!" she shouted.

"Shall we play ball or eat first?" Minnie asked.
"Let's play first, then eat!" Penny said.
"Eat first, then play," said Daisy.
As the girls were trying to decide what to do, a gray cloud passed over the sun and the sky grew dark.

Then....

Drip! Drop! Drip! Drop! Big round raindrops came falling from the sky. Rain dripped on the blanket. Rain dropped on the food.

"There goes our picnic!" said Clarabelle. "This wasn't such a good idea after all."

It rained harder and harder.

SPLISH! SPLASH! The rain poured down.

"Looks like the weather reporter was wrong!" Daisy cried.
"It's probably just an April shower," Minnie said.
"Shower or not, our day is ruined!" Penny complained.

Oh, how awful! My friends are so disappointed! But I think I know how we can still have fun together.

"Well, I guess there's nothing we can do now. We'd better go home. There'll be no picnic today!" Clarabelle said.

Minnie smiled and said, "Maybe there is something we can do! Maybe there will be a picnic."

"You can't stop the rain!" Clarabelle said.

"And our food is ruined!" said Daisy.

"I have an idea," Minnie said. "Let's pack our things and go back to my house."

It rained harder and harder as everyone ran to Minnie's house.

The girls were drenched by the time they got back to the house.

"I'm all wet!" Clarabelle cried.

"I'm cold!" Penny said.

"What an awful, awful day," said Daisy.

"The day isn't over," Minnie answered. "You'll be surprised!"

   "We'd better get out of these wet clothes," Minnie said. "Come with me."

   The girls followed Minnie to the bathroom. They hung up their clothes and wrapped themselves in big fluffy towels.

   Daisy looked in the mirror. The towels reminded her of Hawaiian costumes. She started to dance around the room. "Hey! This is fun!" she shouted.

   "Not as much fun as a picnic!" Clarabelle said.

   Penny danced along with Daisy. "I wish we were in Hawaii where it's warm and sunny!" she said.

Minnie smiled. "I have a surprise for all of you," she said, "but you have to wait here. Don't come down until I call you!"

Minnie took paper, yellow paint, scissors, and some other art supplies with her, then she disappeared down the stairs.

"What's Minnie up to?" asked Penny.

"I don't know," Clarabelle answered. "All I know is there's no picnic."

"We'll soon find out," Daisy said.

When she got downstairs, Minnie
moved the furniture out of the way.

Then she spread the
blanket on the floor
and placed potted
plants all around it.

Next she sliced pineapples,
bananas, and other fruits
and arranged them on
a pretty tray.

Then she went to work making bright crepe-paper flowers.

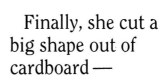

Finally, she cut a big shape out of cardboard —

and painted it yellow.

Soon everything was ready, and Minnie called her friends. When they came down, they could hardly believe their eyes.

"It looks like Hawaii!" Daisy shouted. "We're going to have a luau! A Hawaiian picnic!"

"What a wonderful surprise!" Penny said. "Minnie kept her promise after all."

"It is a wonderful surprise," said Clarabelle, "but a picnic isn't a picnic without sunshine."

Just then, Daisy noticed something moving behind one of the curtains. She ran over and pulled the curtain aside.

There was Minnie holding a big, bright yellow sun high above the picnic. Minnie twirled around so that everyone could see its warm and sunny face.

I'm so happy I thought of a way to have our picnic after all. Aren't you?

"You see," Minnie said, "when good friends are together, every day is filled with sunshine."

"Right again, Minnie!" Daisy agreed. "Now, let's eat!"

Everybody sat down and enjoyed their delicious picnic lunch.

Then they stretched out on the blanket and told stories and secrets and jokes. They made faces and giggled and had a wonderful time. And Minnie took pictures of all her friends.

Soon it stopped raining. The clothes were dry, and it was time to go home. All the girls gave Minnie a great big hug, and she gave them each a picture of their rainy-day picnic.

"We'll keep these pictures forever," said Penny. "They will remind us of the wonderful friend you are and of the best rainy-day picnic ever."